GREAT ILLUSTRATED CLASSICS

MOBY DICK

Herman Melville

adapted by
Shirley Bogart

Illustrations by
Pablo Marcos Studio

BARONET BOOKS, New York, New York

GREAT ILLUSTRATED CLASSICS

edited by
Malvina G. Vogel

Contents

About the Author

When Herman Melville was born in 1819 in New York City, the Melvilles had a successful importing business. But the business failed, and Herman's father died when Herman and his seven brothers and sisters were just children. This made it necessary for Herman to go to work after only a few months of high school.

He educated himself, though, by reading and later said that his Harvard and his Yale—the great schools of learning—were his whaling ships.

Herman tried his hand at many types of work—farming, clerking, and teaching. But everything seemed dull to him except the ever-inviting sea. He was only 18 when he first signed up on a vessel going to and from Liverpool, England, and only 21 when he sailed on a whaler from New Bedford, Massachusetts, to the Pacific.

After 18 months of serving under a cruel captain, Herman jumped ship at the Marquesas Islands in the Pacific. Here, he was captured by cannibals, but he managed to escape on an Australian whaler, and returned to the United States to join the Navy.

Melville turned to writing in the 1840s, and all of his adventures found their way into the books and stories he wrote before his death in 1891. Some of his most famous books are *Typee, Omoo, Billy Budd,* and *Moby Dick.*

Anyone who reads *Moby Dick* can tell that its author spent a lot of time at sea. Only someone who had actually worked on a whaler could show such fantastic knowledge of the day-to-day details of this rough and exciting life.

But if he had written nothing else, Herman Melville's name would live in the hearts of those who love great adventure books—because of his masterpiece, *Moby Dick.*

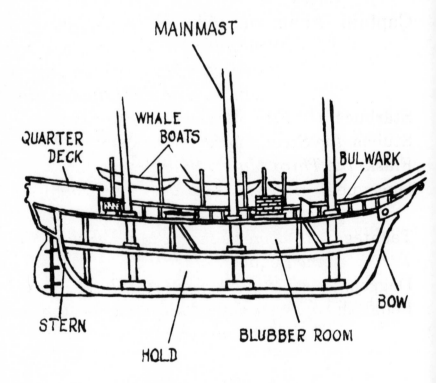

Cross-Section of a Whaling Ship

People You Will Read About

Ishmael, *a young school teacher who goes to sea on a whaling ship and lives to tell the story*

Captain Ahab, *the fanatic one-legged commander of the* Pequod *who swears vengeance on a gigantic white whale who crippled him*

Starbuck, *the First Mate on the* Pequod

Stubbs, *the Second Mate on the* Pequod

Flask, *the Third Mate on the* Pequod

Queequeg, *a New Zealand harpooner and cannibal who befriends Ishmael*

Tashtego, *an American Indian harpooner on the* Pequod

Daggoo, *an African harpooner on the* Pequod

Fedallah, *a mysterious Philippine Indian who makes strange predictions*

Moby Dick, *the Great White Whale with almost human-like intelligence*

The Sea Restores Ishmael's Spirits.

CHAPTER 1

A Strange Roommate

Call me Ishmael. I am a schoolmaster, and whenever life got me down, I would leave my job and head for one special place. When my spirits needed restoring, I could always count on the sea.

I don't mean I'd travel as a passenger. No, for me the way to escape the closeness of my home town of Manhatto, New York, was to go to sea as a plain seaman. I liked the exercise, I liked getting paid instead of having to pay, plus I liked satisfying my yen for seeing faraway places.

This time, though, I decided that instead of signing up on a merchant vessel, I'd go on a whaling ship that would sail from that original home of whaling, Nantucket, an island off the coast of Massachusetts. I had to go to New Bedford first, then take a small boat to Nantucket.

I arrived in New Bedford on a bitter cold Saturday night in December, only to get some bad news. The last boat for Nantucket had just left, and there wouldn't be another until Monday morning. I hadn't counted on the extra expense of staying in New Bedford two nights, but I had no choice. So I began to look around for a low-cost inn.

Since the ones I passed seemed too cheerful and attractive for my pocket, I kept on walking in the icy wind. Finally, near the dock, I came to a run-down gabled house. Its sign creaked as it swung over the ramshackle door. Under a picture of a jet spray were the words

Looking For a Low-Cost Inn

"The Spouter Inn—Peter Coffin."

"Not very appealing," I thought, "but better than being outdoors this frosty night."

The first thing I saw as I entered the inn was a dismal picture of a sinking ship and a whale. One wall was hung with all kinds of frightening weapons—clubs, spears, whaling lances, and rusty harpoons. The entrance to the bar was formed by the arch of a whale's open mouth, and the wrinkled bartender seemed to be mixing drinks inside the whale's fierce jaws.

The landlord said that he was full up, but that if I wanted to stay, I would have to share a bed with a harpooner. I didn't like the idea, but I knew that sharing rooms was a common practice in small-town inns. I told the landlord that if I had no choice, I might put up with half of a decent man's blanket.

All through supper I watched for the harpooner to arrive, but he did not appear. I

Mixing Drinks Inside a Whale's Jaws

dreaded the thought of sleeping in a strange bed in a strange town with a total stranger—especially a rough harpooner. I kept a worried eye on the door until midnight, but there was still no sign of him.

"Landlord," I finally said, "where is he? And what sort of man is he, to keep such late hours?"

"Generally he's the early bird what catches the worm,' explained the landlord. "But tonight he's out a-peddlin. Must be havin' trouble sellin' his head."

"His *what*?" I shouted.

"Be easy," said the landlord. "This harpooner has just arrived from the South Seas with a lot of embalmed shrunken heads from New Zealand. Great curios, you know. He's sold 'em all but one, and I told him it wouldn't do to be sellin' human heads about the streets tomorrow, when folks is goin' to church."

"He sounds like a dangerous man," I cried.

Waiting For the Harpooner

"He pays regular," said the landlord, lighting a candle. "And that's all that concerns me. Now come along and I'll take you to your room."

A crazy old sea-chest stood in the small cold room, and in the middle was a bed big enough for four harpooners. There was no other furniture but a rough shelf and an old wooden chair. A seaman's bag sat on the floor, and a tall harpoon stood beside the bed.

I was restless for a while after the landlord left. At last, I slid off into a light doze.

Suddenly, a heavy footstep in the passageway awakened me, and I saw a gleam of light come into the room.

"Lord save me!" I thought. "It must be the head-peddler."

I lay perfectly still, watching a shadowy figure cram the horrible New Zealand head into the sea-bag. He flipped his heavy sea-coat on the chair, reached into the bag, and

A Shadowy Figure Enters the Room.

took out what looked like a tomahawk. I couldn't see the man's face for a while, but when I did, I froze.

The face was of a dark-purplish color, stuck all over with large blackish-looking squares. And when he pulled off his hat, I came close to crying out in surprise. There was no hair on his head—none but a small twisted scalp-knot, a hank of long hair that had been left in the center when the rest was shaved off. His bald purplish head looked for all the world like a mildewed skull.

Had the stranger not stood between me and the door, I would have bolted out of the room in a frightened rush. But I just lay there waiting, silently examining the rest of him.

His chest, arms, and back were checkered like his face, and his legs were so covered with tattoos, they resembled a parade of dark green frogs running up the trunks of young palm trees.

A Tomahawk!

The stranger reached over to where he had thrown his heavy sea-coat, and from the pocket he took a little hunchbacked figure— a worshipping idol, a handful of wood shavings, a candle, and a bit of ship's biscuit. These he set on the fireplace. Then he lit a kind of sacrificial flame, burned the biscuit and seemed to make a polite offering of it to the little figure. His face twitched in an unnatural manner, and he made strange noises in his throat. He seemed to be worshipping this figure in some sort of ceremony. I could only watch in fascination.

The Stranger Worships a Figure.

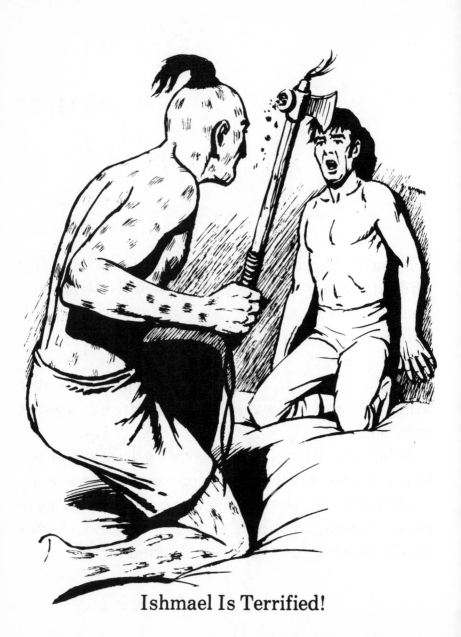

Ishmael Is Terrified!

CHAPTER 2

A Friend for Life

Finally the stranger put out the little fire and stuffed the tiny idol back in his coat pocket. I was thinking of speaking out, but before I could, he suddenly popped the tomahawk-shaped object between his teeth, brought a match up to it, and puffed out a huge cloud of tobacco smoke. Then he jumped into bed.

When I called out, he grunted in surprise. But I stammered and rolled toward the wall.

He began to shout and wave the tomahawk-pipe, spreading hot ashes all around. I was terrified he'd cut me or set the bed on fire.

"Who-ee debil you?" he yelled. "Speak-ee, or dam-me, I kill-ee!"

I shouted for the landlord who, thank Heaven, arrived quickly with a light in his hand.

"Don't be afraid," he said, grinning from the open door. "Queequeg wouldn't harm a hair of your head."

"Why didn't you tell me the harpooner was a cannibal?" I roared.

"I thought ye knowed. Didn't I tell ye he was out peddlin' heads?" He turned to Queequeg. "Look here. This man sleepee you— you sabbee?"

"Me sabbee," Queequeg grunted, puffing away at his pipe. He politely turned the cover back and motioned for me to get into bed.

I took a good look at him and realized that under all that paint he was really a good, sober man. He probably had as much reason to be afraid of me as I had to fear him.

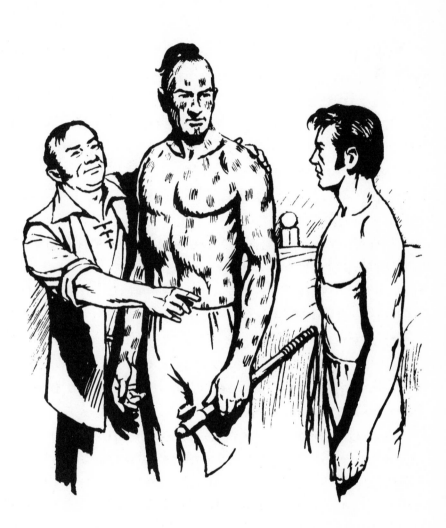

"Don't Be Afraid of Queequeg."

"Okay, landlord," I said, "but tell him to put the tomahawk away and stop smoking in bed. I ain't insured for fire."

Queequeg readily agreed and rolled way over to one side, as if to say, "You've nothing to fear from me."

"Good night, landlord," I said. "You may go."

The next morning, Queequeg courteously signaled that he would dress first and let me have the room to myself. My roommate was polite, while I was the rude one. I couldn't help staring as he put on his tall beaver hat first, then got under the bed to put on his boots in privacy. After this, he crawled out to put on his pants and shirt.

Next he took a wet piece of soap and began to lather his face. I wondered what kind of razor he had and soon found out, much to my surprise. He slipped the harpoon head off its long pole, sharpened it on his boot, and

Queequeg Puts On His Boots in Privacy.

vigorously scraped away at his cheeks. I found this amazing at the time, but I would not find this so amazing later on, when I learned how sharp these fine steel harpoon-heads are kept.

At breakfast, I was expecting to hear exciting sea stories from all the experienced whalers, but they were silent, bashful bears. Queequeg kept pretty busy, though. He'd brought his harpoon along and, ignoring the hot rolls and coffee, reached the harpoon across the breakfast table to spear one beefsteak after another, all as rare as could be.

Later I found myself alone in the public room with him. I watched as he picked up a heavy book from the table and slowly counted the pages in his strange language. After every fifty pages, he'd stop and whistle in astonishment at how many pages there were. Then he'd go on counting.

I wondered to myself why he wasn't more friendly with the other seamen at the inn.

Queequeg Spears the Beefsteak.

But on second thought, I liked him for it. Here was a man 20,000 miles away from his home in New Zealand, in a place as foreign to him as if he'd landed on the planet Jupiter.

Yet he managed to keep himself at ease, content with his own companionship. I felt myself drawn to him. So I pulled up my bench and tried my best to talk to him. He asked me if we'd be sharing a room again that night. When I said yes, he looked pleased, as if I'd complimented him by not arranging for a change.

I tried to explain a bit about the book he was holding—what printing was and what the pictures in it meant. When I suggested we smoke, he produced his tobacco pouch and tomahawk-pipe. We passed the pipe back and forth a few times.

When our smoke was over, he pressed his forehead against mine, clasped me around the waist, and said that we were "married"—

Ishmael Explains What Printing Is.

which in his country's language meant that we were now best friends and he would die for me if necessary. Here in America, of course, we don't trust people so quickly. Close friendships don't form so fast. I felt, though, that in the case of this innocent savage, the old rules just didn't apply.

In our room, after supper and another friendly smoke, he made me a present of his embalmed head. Then he took his tobacco pouch and, groping under the tobacco, took out some thirty dollars in silver. This he divided into two parts and insisted that half was mine. I tried to refuse, but he picked them up and forced them into my pocket.

Then he took out the little hunchbacked figure he had used in his ritual the previous night and made signs that he wanted me to join him in his ceremony. This posed a problem for me. As a good Christian, I knew worshipping idols was against my religion. But

A Present of an Embalmed Head

then I got to thinking—could my great God, mighty ruler of all heaven and earth, be jealous of a little piece of wood? And doesn't God really want us all to do for our fellow men what we want them to do for us? So I lit the fire, offered the figure some burnt biscuit, and bowed once or twice. This done, I went to bed.

With both of us wide awake early in the morning, Queequeg began to talk about his background. "Queequeg born on Kokovoko—small-ee island in South Pacific," he explained. "Queequeg father King, and uncle High Priest of island. Queequeg be King when old father dies. But Queequeg have see Christian world first and bring back great improvements to his people.

"So when whaling ship land on Kokovoko, Queequeg beggee captain take him aboard. Captain say no, but Queequeg not give up. Paddle his canoe to narrow strait ship must enter, sink canoe, climb up side of ship, and

Ishmael Offers the Figure a Burnt Biscuit.

throw himself on deck. Again captain say no. But when he see chief's son ready to die, he let Queequeg stay on board. There, Queequeg learn-ee whaling."

"Do you plan to go back soon and take over your throne?" I asked.

"Queequeg watch-ee how sailors behave and learn-ee that even Christians be wicked," he said. "Now Queequeg feel he not fit carry on line of thirty pure kings before him. At least not till-ee some day, when Queequeg feel clean once more."

"What will you do now?" I asked.

"Queequeg sail again," he said firmly.

"I plan to sign on a whaling ship out of Nantucket," I told him.

"Den Queequeg go with friend and sign-ee on same ship."

I was glad for two reasons. Queequeg was my friend, and he was an experienced harpooner. As such, he would be a good teacher for me on my first whaling voyage.

Queequeg Begged to Stay on Board.

What To Do with a Wheelbarrow?

CHAPTER 3

The Mysterious Captain Ahab

The next morning Queequeg and I borrowed a wheelbarrow and brought our things to the dock. He told me that the first time he had seen a wheelbarrow he didn't know what to do with it, so he fastened his sea-chest to it and carried the whole thing on his shoulders.

"Didn't people laugh?" I asked.

"All peoples laugh-ee at different ways," he replied. "I tell-ee you nother story. Sea captain him visiting Kokovoko Island... he be tell-ee come along wedding Queequeg sister. High Priest him take big bowl and dippee fingers in for bless coconut juice before it-give-ee to guests. Captain not sabbee. Him wash-ee hands in juice.... What you tink now? Tink Queequeg people not laugh?"

"Yes, Queequeg," I said. "I suppose they did."

By now we had reached the *Moss*, a small ship sailing from New Bedford to Nantucket, and we went on board. Some of the passengers started to make fun of Queequeg. One in, particular got him angry. Dropping his harpoon, Queequeg lifted the rude man and threw him in the air. As he was coming down, Queequeg gently tapped his back in the middle of his somersault, and the fellow landed on his feet. Queequeg then turned his back to him and lit his tomahawk-pipe.

The man complained to the captain, who came running. "What in thunder do you mean by that? You might have killed the chap!" he shouted.

Queequeg Lifts a Rude Man in the Air.

"What him say?" asked Queequeg calmly.

"The captain say you near kill-ee that one there," I said, pointing to the shivering man.

Queequeg's face took on a look of contempt. "Kill-ee him?" he said. "Him small-ee fish. Queequeg no kill-ee small-ee fish; Queequeg kill-ee big whale!"

"I'll kill-ee you, cannibal," roared the captain, "if you try any tricks again. So watch out."

But it was the captain's turn to watch out. Something had gone wrong in raising the mainsail. The boom, or long low pole that keeps the sail stretched out, was now swinging from side to side, making huge sweeps of the deck. On one sweep, it brushed the rude character overboard, then continued to swing back and forth, looking like it would go on like that until it snapped. Everybody just stood frozen to the deck, not knowing what to do.

Everybody except for Queequeg. First he

The Boom Pushes the Man Overboard.

dropped to his knees and crawled under the path of the boom to a rope. He tied one end of it to the bulwarks, or sides of the upper deck. The other end he flung out like a lasso and caught the boom as it went over his head. All was steady.

Then he stripped off his shirt and made a perfect dive into the freezing, foamy water. We couldn't see anyone but Queequeg swimming around. Suddenly he disappeared underwater and then surfaced, stroking with one arm and dragging a limp form with the other.

The rude man was saved, the captain apologized to Queequeg, and I made up my mind never to leave my best friend's side.

I had to part from him for a short while though, once the Moss reached Nantucket. Back in our room in New Bedford, Queequeg had insisted that the little idol he carried about—Yojo was its name—had given him a

A Perfect Dive into the Freezing Water

message. It had said that I, alone, was to pick out the whaling ship for us to sign up with.

After checking out the ships ready for a three-year whaling trip, I chose the Pequod—a small, old-fashioned vessel. I told a sun-tanned, wrinkled gentleman I met on board that I wanted to sign up. He introduced himself as Captain Peleg, one of the two owners of the *Pequod* .

"What takes thee a-whaling?" asked Captain Peleg. "I want to know why before I think of shipping ye."

"Well, sir, I want to see what whaling is," I explained.

"Have ye ever clapped an eye on Captain Ahab?"

"Who's Captain Ahab, sir?"

"He's the captain of this ship. Why don't ye take a good look at him before ye tie yourself up in whaling?... Ye'll find him when ye see a man with only one leg."

Going Aboard the *Pequod* to Sign Up

"Did he lose the other while whaling?" I asked.

"Did he lose it while whaling, ye ask? Young man, it was crunched off by the biggest sea monster that ever chipped a boat!"

The old captain's story didn't make me change my mind, and I finally convinced him I was determined to sign on. When I told him about Queequeg, he said to bring him along. Just as I was about to leave, I remembered I hadn't met the ship's captain.

"Where can I find Captain Ahab?" I asked.

"Why do ye want to see him? It's enough that you're shipped."

"Yes, but I still would like to see him."

"Well, don't count on it," said Captain Peleg. "He's sick. ... No, he isn't exactly sick, but he's not well, either. Anyhow, he won't always see me, so I don't think he'll see ye. He's kind of moody, but a good man, a good man. ... Named after a king in the Bible, ye

Describing the Whale

know."

"Yes, but wasn't the biblical Ahab a wicked king who was killed?" I asked.

"Don't ever say that on board the *Pequod*! Ahab didn't choose his name. I know Captain Ahab. He may have lost his mind a little on his last trip home, but that was because of the pain in his leg stump. And remember, he's got a young wife and a son. Don't judge him by his wicked name."

I left, puzzling over in my mind all that Captain Peleg had said about the mysterious Captain Ahab.

Ishmael Is Puzzled About Captain Ahab.

Peleg Doesn't Want a Cannibal Aboard.

CHAPTER 4

Setting Sail

As we boarded the *Pequod,* Captain Peleg stopped us. "Ye hadn't told me Queequeg was a cannibal," he said in a shocked voice. "We don't allow any pagans unless they're converted. Do ye have Queequeg's papers to show he is a Christian?"

"He's a member of the First Congregational Church," I said.

"Ye mean the one run by Deacon Coleman? I pass it every Sunday and never once seen him. Are ye trying to put one over on me?"

"Listen," I said, "he's a born member and a

deacon himself."

"Come on, now," said the captain. "What church are ye talking about?"

Feeling myself pushed, I said, "The great First Congregational Church of the World— the church that you and I and every mother's son worships in. We all belong to that church. We may have a few small differences, but in the one grand belief in God, we all join hands."

"I never heard a better sermon," said Peleg. "Maybe ye ought to ship as a missionary. But tell me, has your friend Quohog ever stuck a fish?"

Queequeg understood the question and took it as a test. He jumped onto the bulwarks and from there onto the bow of one of the hanging boats. Raising his harpoon, he called out, "Cap'n, you see him small-ee drop tar on water dere? Well, s'pose-ee him one whale eye. Well, den! "

Taking sharp aim, Queequeg darted the

Queequeg Shows Off His Skill with a Harpoon.

harpoon and struck the shiny tar spot out of sight.

"Now," said Queequeg matter-of-factly as he hauled in the line, "s'pose-ee him whale eye. Dat whale dead."

It didn't take Peleg long to sign him on. Instead of writing his name, Queequeg copied a sign he had tattooed on his arm.

We had just left the *Pequod* and were ambling along the street when we were stopped by a stranger. He was shabbily dressed and had a badly pockmarked face.

"Shipmates, have ye signed on that ship?" he asked, his finger pointing to the *Pequod* like a fixed bayonet.

"Yes," I said. "We have just signed the papers."

"Anything in those papers about your *souls*?"

"About our *what*?" I asked in amazement.

"Well, maybe ye haven't got any," said the

"Have Ye Signed on That Ship?"

stranger. "But *he's* got enough to make up for the lack in other chaps, he does... Old Thunder."

"Who's Old Thunder?" I asked.

"Captain Ahab, of course. What do ye know about him?"

Although the bedraggled stranger's mind seemed to have slipped a bit, I answered him. "He knows his whaling and he's a good captain."

"Both true—but what about the other things?... Oh well, never mind. Your names are on the papers already. Some sailors or other must go with him, I guess. God pity 'em. Good morning, and the heavens bless ye."

"You can't fool us," I said. "It's easy to look like you have a secret."

"Mornin' to ye. Mornin'," he said as he turned to go.

"Come on, Queequeg. Let's leave this crazy man. But tell us your name, will you,

The Stranger's Warning

stranger?"

"Elijah," he answered.

Queequeg and I walked away, both agreeing that the ragged old sailor was a phony. But that name Elijah made me think. The Elijah in the Bible had been a prophet who had warned of bad things to come.

We waited a few days while the *Pequod* was being loaded with all the supplies needed for a three-year voyage. I kept asking for Captain Ahab, but always got the same answer—he was better and would be coming on board soon. When we received word that we'd be setting sail, I still hadn't met him. I felt uneasy about spending three years serving a captain I'd never seen.

It was about six in the morning when Queequeg and I arrived at the wharf. I thought I saw some sailors running in front of us, but I couldn't be sure in the morning mist.

"Stop!" called a voice, and we each felt a

Seeing Sailors Run Toward the Ship

hand on our shoulder. It was Elijah.

"Ye ain't goin' aboard?" he asked.

"We are, but it's no concern of yours," I answered.

"Did ye see some men goin' toward the ship just now?" he asked.

"Yes, but it was too dim to make out who they were," I said.

"Very dim, very dim. Well, see if ye can find 'em now.... Mornin' to ye. Shan't see ye again, I guess...." With those final cracked words, he left.

The *Pequod* hoisted anchor and set sail under Captain Peleg. When we were out of the bay and on the ocean, a small sailboat came to take him back to the shore. Queequeg and I still hadn't set eyes on Captain Ahab, but we got to know the other members of the crew.

Starbuck, the Chief Mate, was a thin, steady man who seemed to me brave, but in a practical way. Having lost his father and his

Captain Peleg Goes Back to Shore.

brother at sea, Starbuck was not a man to take foolish risks.

The Second Mate was Stubb, an easygoing, fearless man, and a continual smoker. You'd as soon expect to see his face without his nose, as to see it without his little black pipe.

Flask was the Third Mate. This short, stubby sailor seemed to be out hunting whales just for the fun of it. The long voyage around Cape Horn at the southern tip of South America was only a jolly joke to him.

Each of these three mates commanded one of the *Pequod*'s small whaling boats, and each had his own harpooner. Chief Mate Starbuck had chosen Queequeg; Tashtego, a Massachusetts Indian, worked with Stubb, the Second Mate; and Daggoo, a gigantic African, was Flask's harpooner.

With the three mates taking turn at command, nothing was seen of Captain Ahab. Then, a few days after we'd left Nantucket, I

The Three Harpooners

came on deck at the call of the afternoon watch. With a sudden shiver, I saw... *him*.

Standing there so grimly, Captain Ahab reminded me of a bronze statue, tall and broad of form. A thin white scar threaded its way out from his gray hair and continued right down his face and neck till it disappeared inside his clothing. That scar looked like the line in a great tree which had been struck by lightning, but was still alive... and branded. One of his legs was ivory, made from the smooth bone of a whale's jaw.

How could he stand so firmly on that ivory leg with the ship rocking as it was, I wondered. Then I saw the explanation. A half-inch hole had been drilled on each side of the officers' quarter-deck. His bone leg fit in that hole, keeping him erect as he stared silently out beyond the ship's ever-pitching prow.

Captain Ahab seemed to be troubled by some mighty woe.

Captain Ahab

Ahab Shouts at Stubb.

CHAPTER 5

"Death to Moby Dick!"

As our ship moved southward and we hit warmer weather, Captain Ahab came on deck more often, either to stand with his leg anchored in the hole or to sit on a stool fixed the same way. He'd often pace the deck unsteadily. Sometimes the restless pounding of his leg upon the wooden deck at night would keep us awake.

When Stubb half-jokingly asked him to cover the ivory the next night he felt like pacing the deck, Ahab turned on him.

"Down, dog, and to thy kennel!" he shouted.

Stubb was speechless for a moment. "I am

not used to being spoken to in that way, sir. I do not like it, sir," he said.

"Then be called ten times a donkey and be gone, or I'll clear the world of thee!" Ahab advanced toward him threateningly.

Stubb retreated, muttering to the men as he walked by, "I don't know whether to strike him or pray for him. Is he mad? And what can be on his mind that lets him stay in bed only three hours a day? And even then he doesn't sleep. The steward says his bed's always rumpled and his pillow's hot as a baked brick. He's full of riddles, that one."

One morning after breakfast, Ahab's steady step was heard as usual. The dents made by his ivory leg on the deck looked deeper than usual, as if his nervous steps that morning left deeper marks. His forehead, too, was lined, as if one constant thought had kept him always awake.

All day long he paced the deck. Suddenly,

"Is He Mad?"

near the close of day, he stopped by the bulwarks and commanded Starbuck to send
everybody aft. The mate was surprised at
this strange order for the crew to gather at
the rear of the ship.

Ahab continued to pace, unmindful of our
curious whispering. Finally, he cried out,
"What do ye do when ye see a whale, men?"

"Sing out for him!" came the answer.

"Good! And what do ye do next, men?"

"Lower away and go after him!"

"And what tune do ye row to, men?"

"A Dead Whale or a Stove Boat!"

Ahab's face grew happier and more approv-
ing with every shout. Then he took out a
bright coin and called for a hammer.

"Look ye. D'ye see this Spanish ounce of
gold? Whosoever of ye sights a white-headed
whale with a wrinkled brow and a crooked
jaw... whosoever of ye sights that white-
headed whale with three holes punctured in

A Spanish Ounce of Gold

his starboard fluke. . . look ye, whosoever of ye sights that same white whale, he shall have this gold ounce, my boys!"

"Hurrah, hurrah!" the seamen shouted as Ahab nailed the gold coin to the mast.

"It's a white whale, I say," continued Ahab. "Look sharp for white water. If ye see but a bubble, sing out."

All this time Tashtego, Daggoo, and Queequeg had been looking on with more interest and more surprise than the rest of the crew. At the mention of the wrinkled brow and crooked jaw they had started, as if each were touched by some past memory.

"Captain Ahab," said Tashtego, "that white whale must be the one called Moby Dick."

"Aye. Do ye know the white whale then, Tash?"

"Does he move his tail from side to side before he goes down?" asked Tashtego.

"And has he an odd spout and is he mighty

Ahab Nails the Gold Coin to the Mast.

quick, Captain Ahab?" asked Daggoo.

"And he have two, three iron in him hide too, Captain," cried Queequeg. "All twisketee, like so." And Queequeg circled his hand round and round. "Like so. . . . "

"Corkscrew!" cried Ahab. "Aye, Queequeg, the harpoons lie all twisted in him. Aye, Daggoo, his spout is a big one. Aye, Tashtego, and he moves his tail from side to side. . . he fantails before going down. Death and devils! Men, it *is* Moby Dick ye have seen—Moby Dick, Moby Dick!"

"Captain Ahab," said Starbuck, "was it not Moby Dick that took off thy leg?"

"Aye, it was that cursed White Whale who gave me this dead stump I stand on now. And I'll chase him round the Cape of Good Hope and round Cape Horn and round the flames of Hell before I give up. And this is what ye have shipped for, men, to chase that White Whale over all sides of the earth until he spouts black

"That Whale Gave Me This Dead Stump."

blood and rolls over! What say ye, men? Are ye brave enough to join hands in it now?"

"Aye, aye!" shouted the harpooners and seamen.

"God bless ye, men," Ahab half-sobbed, half-shouted. "Steward, go draw some rum for the men." Then seeing Starbuck standing silently, Ahab asked, "Why do ye look so glum, Starbuck? Won't *ye* chase Moby Dick?"

"I am game for his crooked jaw and for the jaws of Death too, if it comes from the *whaling* business we follow. But I came here to hunt whales, not for my captain's revenge!"

Starbuck, alone, opposed the captain, but of course he would not rebel. "God save me! God save us all!" he murmured softly.

Ahab ordered a big pewter drinking mug filled with rum. "Drink and pass!" he cried, handing it to the nearest seaman. "Long swallows, men. 'Tis hot as Satan's hoof. . . . Well done, almost drained. Steward, refill!"

"Drink and Pass!"

Next, he called for the three mates to come forth. "Cross your lances that I may revive a noble custom of my fisherman fathers," he said, gripping the three irons at their crossed center. He gazed deeply from Starbuck to Stubb and from Stubb to Flask, as if to fire them with his own fiery enthusiasm. The mates looked away from his strong, mystic stare.

"Down with your lances." Then Ahab turned to Queequeg, Tashtego, and Daggoo. "And now, my three valiant harpooners, detach the poles from your weapons, men."

Queequeg, Tashtego, and Daggoo slipped off the iron tips of their harpoons and turned them upside down, with the hollow openings facing up.

Filling them like goblets, Ahab ordered, "Drink, ye harpooners. Drink and swear— Death to Moby Dick! God hunt us all if we do not hunt Moby Dick to his death!"

Ahab Grips the Three Irons.

Ishmael Learns About Whales.

CHAPTER 6

The Phantom Five

I began to pick up all sorts of information about whales in general and about Moby Dick, in particular. The most prized of all whales is the sperm whale, because of its valuable spermaceti—a white, waxlike substance taken from the oil in the sperm whale's head. Spermaceti lights the lamps of the world and is an important ingredient in making perfume.

As for Moby Dick, I learned he could be spotted from a great distance because he differed from most other sperm whales. Not only did he have a peculiar snow-white wrinkled forehead and a high white hump, but the rest of his huge body was so streaked and spotted with the same white color, that he gained the nickname of "The White Whale."

Moby Dick was known to swim frantically away from a boat lowered by a whaling ship to chase him. But he only pretended to be frightened. Suddenly he would turn around and bear down on his pursuers, either breaking their boat to splinters or driving them back in terror to their ship.

Once, a captain went at Moby Dick with three boats. All three were shattered by the whale. Seeing his men spinning about in little whirlpools of the sea, the captain grabbed a small knife with a six-inch blade and dashed at Moby Dick's heart like some wild man in a duel. That captain was Ahab. It was at that moment that the whale swept its curved lower jaw beneath Ahab and cut off his leg!

From that moment on, Ahab wanted revenge against the whale, for to Ahab all the

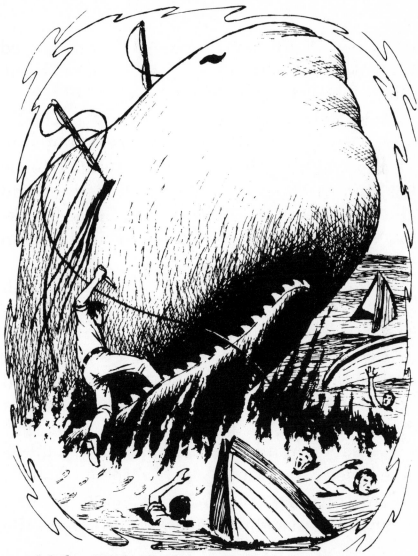

Moby Dick Had Cut Off Ahab's Leg.

evil of the world was rolled into this one crea-
ture. I marveled that he had managed to
make the crew share his hatred and even
take on *his* enemy as their own.

One still moonlit night, we were standing
in line passing buckets to fill the scuttle
butt—a barrel which holds the fresh water
for the day's use. Suddenly, one of the seamen whispered to another, "Hsst! Did you
hear that noise?"

"What noise?"

"There it is again, under the hatches. It
sounded like a cough."

"Be still, shipmate, will ye? It's the three
soaked biscuits ye ate for supper turning over
inside ye—nothing else. Now hand over the
bucket."

"Ye can grin all you like," said the seaman.
"We'll see what turns up. There's somebody
below that has not been seen on deck. I
suspect old Ahab knows something about it

Filling the Scuttle Butt

too. I heard Stubb tell Flask one morning that there was something of the sort in the wind."

Nothing came of this mystery for a while. Then Tashtego, who was keeping a watch on the mainmast, sang out, "There she blows! "

I looked up to see where the Indian had sighted a whale. Tashtego stood perched high in the air, his arm stretched out like a wand.

"There she blows! There! There! There!"

"Where? Where?" came excited shouts.

"On the lee-beam, about two miles off! A school of them!"

That meant they were on the side of the ship away from the wind. Instantly, all was commotion.

"Quick, steward!" cried Ahab. "Get me the time, the time! "

Dough-Boy, the steward, hurried below, glanced at the watch, and reported the exact minute to Ahab.

We knew Ahab kept careful notes of where

"There She Blows! There! There! There!"

and when whales had been sighted or captured. Every night he would take from his locker a large wrinkled roll of sea-charts and study the various lines-and shadings, tracing routes with his slow but steady pencil. He studied the currents of all four oceans and the habits of all whales in order to reach one burning goal—*to find and kill Moby Dick!*

Although we were now going after other whales which, after all, was the main business of the *Pequod,* I knew that Ahab's real prey was ever on his mind.

The ship was now kept away from the wind. Three boats were swung over the side and down to the sea. At this exciting instant, we heard a sudden cry. It took every eye away from the whales and directed them with a glare at Ahab. The captain stood on deck surrounded by five dark phantoms who seemed to have appeared out of the air.

These strangers busied themselves,

Ahab Traces Whale Sightings.

noiselessly lowering one of the spare boats.

"All ready there, Fedallah?" called Ahab.

"Ready," came the half-hissed reply from a tall, dark figure with one tooth evilly protruding from steel-like lips. The man wore a rumpled black cotton jacket and pants, and his long white hair was braided and coiled around his head like a turban. The other men had the tiger-yellow color of the Manillas, a tribe of natives from the Phillipine Islands near Australia. Some superstitious sailors believed these natives to be secret spies of the Devil.

"Lower away, then!" shouted Captain Ahab.

Like goats, our men leaped down the rolling ship's side into the three tossed boats below. In the fourth boat, rowed by the five strangers, stood Ahab. He was yelling across the water at Starbuck, Stubb, and Flask to spread out so as to cover a larger area.

Fedallah Watches the Men Lower the Boat.

When, for a minute or so, their two boats came close, Stubb called to Starbuck, "What think you of those five yellow men, sir?"

"Smuggled on board, somehow, before the ship sailed," called Starbuck. "Pull strong, strong, boys!—A sad business, Mr. Stubb. But never mind, it's all for the best!"

"I thought so too. *That's* why he kept going down into the hold so much. The men were hidden there. The White Whale's at the bottom of it. . . . Well, well, can't be helped now—Give way, men! It ain't the White Whale today!"

I silently recalled the mysterious shadows I had seen creeping on board the *Pequod* during the dim Nantucket dawn. I remembered, too, the puzzling hints of that strange man, Elijah. I would have a lot to think about at a time when there would be less excitement. But for now, all everybody wanted to do was close in on those whales.

Starbuck and Stubb Call to Each Other.

Ahab Gives Orders to the Other Boats.

CHAPTER 7

Men Overboard

Ahab's tiger-yellow men seemed all steel and whalebone. Like five strong trip hammers they rose and fell with hard, regular strokes of their oars. Fedallah, at one end of the boat, pulled the harpooner's oar, while at the other end Ahab steadily managed the steering oar.

"Flask!" called Ahab across to the other boat. "Pull out more to leeward, man."

"Aye, aye, sir." Flask swept his great oar round. "Lay back, men!" he shouted. "There she blows right ahead, boys! Roar and pull, my thunderbolts!"

Meanwhile, in one of the other boats, Stubb

was getting his crew to row too, but in a far different and rather funny way. He'd say the most outrageous things to them, but in a tone that was half-angry and half-joking.

"Pull, pull, my little ones!" shouted Stubb. "Why don't you break your backbones, boys? Pay no mind to the five in yonder boat. The more the merrier! Even if they are devils, they are good fellows. Hurrah for the gold cup of sperm oil. The devil fetch ye ragamuffins, ye're all asleep. Wake up and pull! Every mother's son of ye, draw his knife and pull with the blade between his teeth. That's more like it now!"

In another boat, Starbuck's way was different. He'd command with a low, intense whisper, "Pull, pull, my good boys." He'd never say much to his crew, nor they anything at all to him.

It was a sight full of wonder and awe—the roaring waves of the sea, the boats rolling to

"Pull, Pull, My Little Ones."

the top of a watery hill then sliding sled-like down its other side, the windstorm tossing them about. All these amid the cries of the harpooners and the shuddering gasps of the oarsmen. The *Pequod* bore down on her boats with outstretched sails, like a wild mother hen chasing after her screaming brood. It was thrilling!

Starbuck now gave chase to three whales as our boat rushed along in the rising wind and mist. Suddenly he hurled a lightning-bolt whisper to Queequeg. "Stand up!"

Our harpooner sprang to his feet and waited till he heard, "That's his hump. There, there! Give it to him!"

Queequeg's darting iron made a rushing sound... and then there was confusion. An invisible push came at us from the stern, or rear, of our little boat. The sails collapsed, and something rolled and tumbled like an earthquake beneath us, tossing all of us

Giving Chase to the Whales

helter-skelter into the white curdling foam of the sea. The windstorm, the whale, and the harpoon all blended together, and the whale, merely grazed by the iron, escaped.

Swimming about, we managed to pick up our floating oars, climb back into the lonely boat, and tumble to our places. It was no use calling to the other boats. We could not be heard in the storm. We were up to our knees in water, and in the deepening mist the *Pequod* was nowhere to be seen. As the dawn came on, we sat there drenched through and through, shivering cold, and without hope.

It was Queequeg who first jumped to his feet, cupping his hand to his ear. As we listened, we heard a faint creaking. Then, before we knew what was happening, the *Pequod* loomed into view, bearing right down on us!

We jumped into the sea just moments before our boat was crushed beneath the

The *Pequod* Bears Down on the Men.

Pequod's hull. Again we swam for our lives with the seas dashing us against the ship, until at last we were safely taken up on board. We learned that the three other boats had gotten back in time.

"Queequeg," I said, still shaking myself to fling off the water, "my fine friend, does this sort of thing happen often?"

He calmly gave me to understand that yes it did. Stubb and Flask, who were with us, agreed.

Considering that the three men thought nothing of being overturned; considering that they saw nothing unusual in cautious Mr. Starbuck's driving us onto his whale in the teeth of a squall; and considering, too, our captain's mad quest for the White Whale, there was only one sensible thing for me to do.

"Queequeg," I said, "I am going below and make a rough draft of my will. Come along. You shall be my lawyer and advisor."

"Does This Sort of Thing Happen Often?"

"Have Ye Seen the White Whale?"

CHAPTER 8

A Victim of Moby Dick

Southeastward from the Cape of Good Hope, a name which seemed all wrong for that place of tormented seas, howling winds, and leaping waves, we met another ship. It was the *Albatross*, a ship that had been long absent from home, judging from her rusty sides and the long beards of her tatter-dressed sailors.

"Ship ahoy!" Ahab called to the other captain. "Have ye seen the White Whale?"

But as the captain of the *Albatross* put the trumpet to his mouth to answer, it fell out of his hand into the sea, and he couldn't make himself heard. So we passed on.

Not long after, we met another homeward-bound whaler, the *Town-Ho*. This time, Ahab allowed a gam, or exchange of visits. Some *Town-Ho* crewmen who came on board the *Pequod* whispered the secret of their ship to Tashtego. When he later told it to us, it sparked our interest in Moby Dick.

An officer and a sailor on the *Town-Ho* had gotten into a fight over an unfair order to sweep the deck. In self-defense, the sailor knocked the mate out. Others got involved, and it became a mutiny.

Steelkilt, the seaman, was about to kill Radney, the Chief Mate, when a call came. Moby Dick had been sighted. Radney's boat was the first one lowered away, and as he stood spear in hand, he was washed overboard. Moby Dick clamped him between his jaws, reared up high, and then plunged down into the water.

Clamped Between Moby Dick's Jaws

When the whale rose again, he had some tatters of Radney's red wool shirt caught in his teeth. All four boats gave chase, but Moby Dick had disappeared.

After hearing the *Town-Ho*'s story, we all had Moby Dick on our minds. Daggoo, who had the look-out, saw a great white mass that kept rising and sinking. "There she breaches, right ahead!" he called. "The White Whale, the White Whale!"

Ahab gave instant commands for lowering. His boat was down ahead of the other three. I watched with interest as a vast, pulpy, cream-colored mass hundreds of yards long and wide came floating on the water. Countless numbers of long arms radiated from its center, curling and twisting like a nest of snakes. It had no visible face or front; it was just a ghostly, shapeless living thing.

As it disappeared again, making a low sucking sound, Starbuck said, "I would

A Vast, Pulpy Mass Floats on the Water.

almost rather have seen and fought Moby Dick than that white ghost."

"What was it, sir?" said Flask.

"The great live squid. There's a superstition that few whaleships that see the squid ever return to their ports to tell of it."

Ahab said nothing. He turned his boat and sailed back to the ship, with the rest of us silently following.

But Queequeg had a different opinion about what seeing the squid meant. "When you see 'quid close by, then you see quick 'perm whale."

The next day was hot, and all of us were drowsy. But sure enough, just as Queequeg had said, all at once we spotted a huge sperm whale lazily swimming along and spouting his jet, like some fat citizen leisurely smoking his pipe on a warm afternoon.

But that pipe was the poor whale's last. As if struck by a magician, all the drowsy men

Queequeg Spots a Sperm Whale.

on the sleepy ship awoke and got busy lowering the boats. Our noise must have alarmed the whale, for he threw his tail forty feet into the air and sank out of sight, like a swallowed-up tower.

Stubb, being nearer than any of the others to where the whale again appeared, counted on having the honor of capturing it.

"Start her, start her like thunderclaps, my men," he ordered. "But keep cool—cucumber's the word. Start her, Tash, my boy."

"Woo-hoo! Wa-hee!" screamed the Indian in reply, raising some old war whoop to the skies.

His wild screams were answered by others just as wild from the other boats.

"Kee-hee! Kee-hee!" yelled Daggoo, straining back and forth in his seat like a tiger pacing in his cage.

"Ka-la! Koo-loo!" howled Queequeg.

The men in Stubb's boat tugged and strained until the welcome cry was heard.

"Woo-Hoo! Wah-Hee!"

"Stand up, Tashtego! Give it to him!"

The harpoon was hurled. The boat now flew through the boiling water like a shark that is all fins. She seemed to pass whole Atlantics and Pacifics as she shot on her way, till at last the whale somewhat slowed his flight and the boat's as well.

"Haul in, haul in!" cried Stubb.

All the men faced round towards the whale and began pulling the boat up to him, while he still towed the boat. Stubb sent dart after dart into the whale's body. Soon a red tide poured from all sides of the monster. The sun, playing upon the bloody water, sent back its reflection into every man's face, so that they all glowed to each other like red men.

"Pull up!" Stubb now cried, and the boat moved along the whale's side. Reaching far over the bow, Stubb slowly churned his long sharp lance into the heart of the whale and kept it there, carefully churning and churning.

Stubb Darts His Harpoon into the Whale.

MOBY DICK

The whale made a last desperate flurry, sending the boat backing out of his mad, boiling spray. Then the spray stopped, and the whale once more rolled out into view, opening and closing his spout hole with sharp, cracking breaths. Streams of red blood shot into the air, then ran down the whale's sides into the sea. His heart had burst.

Stubb took his pipe from his mouth, scattered the dead ashes over the water, and stood thoughtfully eyeing the vast corpse he had just made.

Stubb Eyes the Vast Corpse.

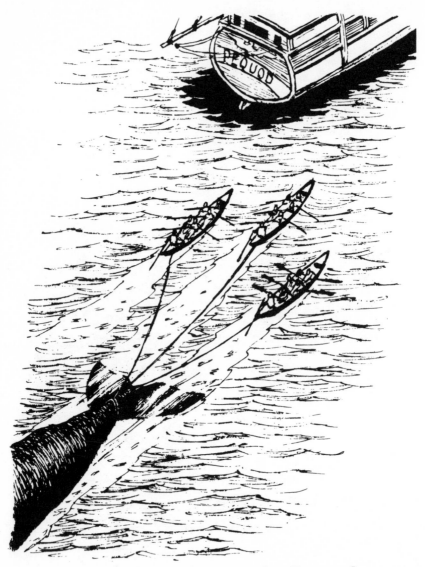

Towing the Prize to the *Pequod*

CHAPTER 9

The Mad Prophet of Doom

Since Stubb's whale had been killed a distance from the ship, three boats now began to tow the prize to the *Pequod*.

So enormous was the mass we moved, that it was dark by the time our thirty-six arms and one hundred eighty fingers finished the job. The sight of the dead whale seemed to pain Ahab, as if he were reminded that Moby Dick was out there, still alive, yet to be killed.

The tremendous body was fastened along the length of our vessel, and Stubb, in a mood of good-natured excitement, ordered whale steak for his dinner.

The next day we began the long hard job of cutting up the dead whale. A foot-thick blanket of blubber, or fat, encircles a whale like a rind encircles an orange. First, Starbuck and Stubb used long spades to dig a hole in the blubber. Next, a huge hook was inserted, and the crew pulled away the first strip. Then the men in the blubber room below got the strip of blubber and began coiling it. This procedure was repeated over and over again until all the blubber was taken care of. A single whale yields enough blubber to make 100 barrels of oil—a lake of liquid that weighs about *ten tons*.

Our work was interrupted by the cry, "Sail ho!" It turned out to be another whaler, the *Jeroboam*, out of Nantucket. When her lowered boat was heading toward us, Starbuck ordered a ladder let down for the visiting captain. But the *Jeroboam's* commander,

Pulling Away the First Strip of Blubber

Captain Mayhew, waved his hand to show they would not be boarding the *Pequod*.

By careful rowing, the *Jeroboam*'s oarsmen kept the boat alongside our ship to make conversation possible. We found out that the reason they wouldn't come on board was because of a bad epidemic on the *Jeroboam*.

Stubb thought he recognized one of the oarsmen, a small, wild-eyed young man with freckled face and much yellow hair. "That must be Gabriel!" said Stubb.

We had heard stories from other crews about this strange man who had been raised as a Shaker. The Shakers, I knew, were an American religious group who shook their bodies as part of their worship.

After signing up as an ordinary seaman, Gabriel had announced himself to be a prophet. Saying he was the angel Gabriel, he had demanded command of the ship. When the captain threatened to land him at the

Oarsmen from the *Jeroboam*

first convenient port, Gabriel began opening
all sorts of mysterious little bottles. He kept
uttering terrible warnings of what would
happen to the crew if the captain carried out
his plan.

So firm and convincing was he, that the
men went to the captain and told him that if
Gabriel were sent from the ship, not a man of
them would remain. They wouldn't let him be
punished in any way either. So Gabriel had
complete freedom of the ship.

When the epidemic broke out on the
Jeroboam, Gabriel had even more power. He
annouced that the plague came about at his
sole command and that it could be stopped
only when it pleased him. The sailors
believed everything he said.

They had all heard about the White Whale
and were eager to hunt him, until Gabriel, in
his wild, babbling way, warned them not to.
He said that Moby Dick was his Shaker God

Gabriel's Warnings!

who had come down in a whale's body.

However, a year later when they encountered the whale, the Chief Mate, Henry
Macey, burned to go after him. Macey finally
persuaded five men to man his boat. As
Gabriel continued to hurl prophecies of doom,
the men got one iron into the sea beast.

Suddenly, a broad white shadow rose from
the water, and the whale, by its quick fan-
ning motion, temporarily took the breath out
of the oarsmen's bodies. The next instant the
unlucky mate was thrown bodily into the air
and, making a long arc in his descent, fell
into the sea some fifty yards away. Not a chip
of the boat was harmed, nor a hair of any
oarsman's head, but the mate sank into the
sea forever.

At this point, Captain Mayhew asked Ahab
if he would hunt Moby Dick if he had the
chance.

"Aye," answered Ahab, whereupon Gabriel

The Mate Was Thrown into the Air.

jumped to his feet and glared up at the old man.

With downward-pointed finger, Gabriel passionately exclaimed, "Think of Macey—the God-insulter, dead, and down there! Beware of the same end!"

Ahab turned aside, saying he just recalled a letter he'd been given in Nantucket for one of the *Jeroboam*'s officers, in case the two ships met at sea. Starbuck went to look for it and soon returned with a damp, worn piece of mail. It was covered with green mold from being stored in a dark locker.

Starbuck took a long pole and slightly split the end to hold the letter as it was passed down.

While Starbuck was splitting the pole, Ahab tried to puzzle out the writing on the envelope.

"Mr. Har—yes, a woman's handwriting, the man's wife, I'll bet—Mr. Harry Macey, Ship

Passing the Letter Down

Jeroboam. Why, it's for Macey, and he's dead!"

"Keep it yourself," cried Gabriel to Ahab. "You're soon going that way too!"

"Curse you!" yelled Ahab. "Captain Mayhew, stand by to receive it."

But Gabriel snatched the letter, poked his knife through it, and hurled it back up to the *Pequod*. It fell right at Ahab's feet.

The Letter Falls at Ahab's Feet.

Readying the Whale for Towing

CHAPTER 10

The Devil on Board?

We next encountered a group of right whales. The oil of these whales was inferior to that of the sperm whales, so I assumed we would not bother hunting any. But I was wrong, for the cry came to lower the boats. Stubb and Flask went in pursuit of the tall spouts.

With one whale harpooned, the two boats pulled up close to his body, and Stubb and Flask took turns plunging in lance for lance until the whale was dead and ready for towing.

"I wonder what the old man wants with

this lump of foul lard," said Stubb.

"Didn't you never hear about the charm?" asked Flask. "Once a ship has a sperm whale's head hoisted on her starboard, or right side, and at the same time a right whale on her larboard, or left side, she can never afterwards capsize."

"Where did you hear that?" asked Stubb.

"From Fedallah," replied Flask. "That ghostly man will charm this ship to a bad end. Doesn't his single tooth look like it's in the head of an evil snake, Stubb?"

"Well, I think Fedallah is the devil in disguise. And the reason we don't see his devil tail is because he coils it up and tucks it in his pocket. "

"Yes. And he sleeps in his boots, don't he?" added Stubb. "That devil Fedallah don't want anyone to see his goat-like hoofs, for they would surely give away his identity. And I'll bet he's even made a bargain with the old man

"Fedallah Is the Devil in Disguise."

too. Got him to swap away his soul if Fedallah promised to surrender Moby Dick to him."

"You must be joking now, Stubb. How can Fedallah do that?"

"I don't know, Flask, but the devil is a strange chap and a wicked one, I tell ye.... But look sharp—we're here. Pull ahead and let's get this whale alongside the ship."

After a while, the two boats, pulling their burden slowly, arrived back at the *Pequod*.

"How old do you think Fedallah is, Stubb?"

To answer, Stubb pointed to the tallest pole on the *Pequod*. "Do you see that mainmast there? Well, say that's the figure *one*. Now take all the hoops on all the barrels stored on this ship. String all those hoops in a row beside that mast and pretend they're *zeroes* following the one. That number wouldn't begin to be Fedallah's age. You couldn't find enough hoops in the world to make zeroes enough."

"But, Stubb, before you said you would like

Fedallah's Age — 10000000000 . . . .

to toss him overboard. If he's going to live forever, what good would it do?"

"Give him a good ducking."

"What if he decided to duck you back and
drown you?"

"I'd like to see him try. Damn the devil,
Flask! Do you suppose I'm afraid of him? If
he makes a fuss, I'll just grab into his pocket
for his tail and wrench it off. Then I'll let him
go sneaking off in shame."

"And what will you do with the tail,
Stubb?"

"Do with it? Sell it for an ox whip when we
get home. What else?"

Flask looked at Stubb with a puzzled
expression. "Do you really mean what you've
been saying all along?" he asked.

"Mean or not mean, here we are at the
ship," replied Stubb.

On the side of the ship away from the
sperm whale, chains were now ready for

Towing the Right Whale to the Ship

securing this right whale.

"Didn't I tell you so?" said Flask, pointing up at the sperm whale's head hoisted up on the Pequod's starboard side. "I told you Fedallah would do that. You'll soon see this one's head hoisted up opposite the other one's."

In good time, what Flask said proved true. When the right whale's head was suspended in place, I saw Fedallah studying it. He was comparing its wrinkles with the lines on the palm of his own hand, as if reading some secret message about the future.

Captain Ahab stood in such a way that Fedallah was completely in his shadow. If Fedallah had any shadow at all, it seemed to lengthen and blend mysteriously with Ahab's.

Fedallah Reads a Secret Message.

Precious Oil in the Whale's Head

CHAPTER 11

Queequeg Does It Again!

As the *Pequod* moved on with the sperm whale's head hanging by its side, a very important piece of work had to be done— the work of removing a treasure.

That treasure is the precious oil which is found within the forehead of the whale in an enormous sac called a case. In cutting off the head of a sperm whale, the cutter has to be careful not to puncture this case, or some of the 500 gallons of oil would be lost.

Tashtego now climbed the main yardarm to the part projecting out over the swinging whale's head. Securing himself to the yardarm, he let himself down with a rope, hand over hand, until he landed on top of the whale's head. One of the crewmen handed him a short-handled spade, but he did not begin to dig at once. Working ever so carefully, he first tapped the skin with the spade to sound its walls.

By the time he found the right spot, an iron bucket, like the kind lowered into a well for water, was attached to one end of the rope and lowered down to him. The other end stretched across the deck and was held by two men.

Tashtego rammed a pole into the bucket and thus lowered it into the whale's case until it disappeared. Then, at his signal, the deck hands pulled on the rope, and up came the filled bucket. On deck it was emptied into a large tub and returned to Tashtego. As the whale's case emptied, the Indian had to ram the pole harder and deeper until, after about a hundred trips, it was some twenty feet

Tashtego Lowers the Bucket.

down inside the whale's forehead.

Suddenly, Tashtego, himself, dropped head-first into the case, and with a horrible gurgling sound. . . disappeared.

"Man overboard!" cried Daggoo, putting a foot into the bucket and calling to be lowered from the deck to the top of the head.

But then, a sharp cracking noise made everyone stop and stare in horror. One of the two huge hooks holding the head tore out. As the head swung sideways, the other hook seemed about to give way too.

With a thunder-boom, the enormous mass dropped into the sea. Daggoo clung to the dangling rope, but poor, buried-alive Tashtego was sinking to the bottom of the sea inside the whale's forehead.

For one swift moment, a naked figure with a sword in hand was seen balancing on the bulwarks. The next instant, a loud splash announced that my brave Queequeg had

The Hook Tears out of the Whale's Head.

dived to the rescue.

In moments, we saw an arm rising strangely from the sea, like an arm reaching out from the grass over a grave.

"Both, both—it is both!" cried Daggoo.

Soon after, we all could see Queequeg boldly striking out with one hand, and clutching the long hair of the Indian with the other.

The rescue, when Queequeg later described it, struck us as being an amazing one. Queequeg had gone down after the sinking whale head and poked some holes near its bottom with his sword.

Upon reaching his hand in, he found he'd grabbed Tashtego's leg. He knew this would mean trouble in trying to tow him in. Thinking and acting fast, he gave the leg a heavy toss. Just as he had hoped, he made the Indian's body do a somersault. With the next try, he reached Tashtego's head and was able to swim in with him in tow.

Queequeg Rescues Tashtego.

"Hast Seen the White Whale?"

CHAPTER 12

On the Trail of the White Whale

"Ship ahoy! Hast seen the White Whale?" The call came from Ahab to a passing ship flying an English flag.

The old man stood on deck with his trumpet to his mouth. Ahab's ivory leg was plainly revealed to the captain of the *Samuel Enderby*. This gentleman was a burly, sunburned, fine-looking man about sixty years old. The empty right sleeve of his jacket streamed behind him.

"Hast seen the White Whale?" Ahab repeated.

"See this?" answered the captain, holding up the right sleeve of his jacket to reveal a white arm made of sperm whale bone. The arm ended in a wooden head like a hammer.

In less than a minute, Ahab's boat was lowered for a visit to the other ship. As the old man climbed aboard, the *Enderby*'s captain advanced, extending his ivory arm in welcome. Ahab crossed it with his ivory leg, calling out, "Aye, aye. Let us shake bones together—an arm and a leg. Was it the White Whale took that arm off?"

"Aye," said the captain. "We had lowered our small boat to hunt some four or five whales. We managed to get our boat fastened to one of them. Suddenly, up from the bottom of the sea came a bouncing great whale with a milky-white head and hump."

"It was he! It was Moby Dick!" shouted Ahab.

"And he had harpoons sticking in near his

Shaking an Arm and a Leg Together

right side," added the captain.

"They were mine! They were my irons!" cried Ahab. "Go on, go on."

"He began snapping furiously at my line."

"Aye. He wanted to free himself. An old trick. I know him."

"The line caught in his teeth, and when we pulled the line, our boat slid to the top of his hump. He was the noblest and biggest whale I ever saw in all my life, so I resolved to capture him in spite of the rage he was in. I jumped into my mate's boat, grabbed the nearest harpoon, and let the old whale have it."

Ahab was listening eagerly.

"Next thing I knew, I couldn't see anything for the black foam, as his tail stuck up right out of the water like a marble steeple. Suddenly, down comes the tail, cutting my boat in two, and then he backs away through the wreck."

"What happened next?" cried Ahab.

"Down Comes the Tail, Cutting My Boat."

"I seized hold of my harpoon pole that was sticking in him. For a moment I clung to that. But the sea dashed me off, and the fish went down like a flash. It was then that the point of that second cursed iron towing along near me caught me here at my shoulder and carried me down—to Hell's flames, I thought for sure."

Ahab stared at the point just below the captain's shoulder where his arm ended.

"All of a sudden, thank the good God, the point tore its way along the flesh down the whole length of my arm. It came out at my wrist, and up I floated."

The ship's doctor who had joined us finished the story. "Aye. A two-foot wound it was. Then it grew worse, and I had to amputate the arm. "

"What became of the White Whale?" asked Ahab, for that was all that interested him.

"We saw him two more times," answered the captain.

"The Iron Caught Me at My Shoulder."

"Couldn't you fasten onto him again?"

"Didn't want to try to. Ain't losing one limb enough?"

The English captain glanced at Ahab's ivory limb. "Don't *you* agree that it's best to leave that whale alone?" he asked.

"Maybe so," said Ahab firmly. "But I'm still going after him. Which way was he heading?"

"He was heading east, I think...." Then turning to Fedallah, the captain whispered, "Good God, is Captain Ahab crazy?"

But Fedallah, putting a finger on his lip, slid over the *Samuel Enderby*'s bulwarks to take our boat's oar. Soon Ahab was standing in the small boat, with his men springing to their oars. The other captain tried to call out to him, but in vain. With his back to the *Enderby*, Ahab stood like a statue until he was alongside the *Pequod*.

Ahab Stands Like a Statue.

Hosing Down the Whale Oil Barrels

CHAPTER 13

Returned to Life

We were carrying a precious cargo by this time—numerous barrels of whale oil which were stored below deck in the hold. In order to protect them, our men hosed them down twice a week with sea water. This had two purposes. First, the water kept the wooden barrels tightly sealed. Second, as the sailors checked the water that was pumped off, they could see if there was any oil mixed with it. In that way, they could detect any serious leakage from the barrels.

The morning after we met the *Enderby,* as

our sailors were pumping the water off the barrels, they discovered much oil rising and mixing with the water. Starbuck rushed down to Ahab's cabin to report it.

"The oil in the hold is leaking, sir. We've got to remove the casks and see where the leak is."

Ahab, who had been studying his charts, whirled around in anger. "We're too close to Japan," he snapped. "Can't waste time tinkering with a pack of old barrels."

"But, sir," argued Starbuck, "we'll be wasting more oil in a day than we can replace in a year. What we've come twenty thousand miles to get is worth saving."

"You're right about that," said Ahab, *"if we get what we've come for."*

"I'm talking about the oil in the hold, sir," said Starbuck calmly.

"And I'm not!" shouted Ahab. "Let it leak. Begone now, Starbuck!"

"But, sir, what will the owners say?"

"The Oil in the Hold Is Leaking."

"Let them stand on Nantucket beach and outyell the storms. Ahab doesn't care. The only real owner of anything is its commander. And Ahab is the Pequod's commander. Now up on deck!"

"But, Captain...." pleaded Starbuck.

Ahab grabbed a loaded gun from the rack and pointed it at his Chief Mate. "There is one God that is lord over this earth, and one Captain that is lord over the Pequod. Get on deck! "

Starbuck, eyes flashing and cheeks on fire, managed to calm himself. As he left the cabin, he turned and said, "You have outraged me, not insulted me, so I'm not going to warn you to beware of Starbuck. You would only laugh at that. But, sir, let Ahab beware of Ahab— you are your own worst enemy!"

After Starbuck had gone, Ahab thoughtfully repeated what he had heard. " 'Let Ahab beware of Ahab'—there's something there."

Ahab Threatens Starbuck.

It would be hard to guess why Ahab finally decided to listen to Starbuck. It could have been a flash of honesty or the thought that it was safer to keep as much good feeling as possible between himself and his chief officer. Anyway, he did order the barrels of whale oil raised and inspected.

While working in the damp, slimy hold at hoisting out the huge barrels of oil, poor Queequeg caught a chill and a terrible fever. Thin and pale, he lay in his hammock wasting away, till there seemed little left of him but his frame and his tattooing. He was on the very edge of the door of death.

One day, Queequeg asked a strange favor. He said that in Nantucket, he had seen certain little dark wood canoes with lids, like on his native isle. He had been told that all whalemen who died in Nantucket were buried in those dark canoes. This idea pleased him. It was like his own people's custom of placing a dead

Queequeg Is Near Death's Door.

warrior in his canoe and letting him float
away into the starry island of the sky.

When the ship's carpenter was told of this
wish, he went straight to Queequeg and mea-
sured him very carefully. Using dark lumber
cut from island trees on a previous trip and
stored on the *Pequod*, he set to work on the
coffin-canoe.

When it was finished, Queequeg called for
his harpoon and had the iron placed in the
coffin, together with one of his boat paddles.
In addition, he requested a flask of fresh
water, a bag of woody earth, and a piece of
sailcloth rolled up for a pillow. When it was
all set up, he had himself lifted into his final
bed for a tryout. He lay there with his arms
crossed and the little god Yojo on his breast.
Then he gave the signal to be returned to his
hammock.

But having made all these preparations for
death and having found the coffin a good fit,

Queequeg Tries Out His Coffin.

Queequeg suddenly got better, as if he'd changed his mind about dying.

Now he used his coffin for a sea-chest, emptying into it his canvas bag of clothes. He spent many spare hours carving on the lid all kinds of strange figures and drawings, mostly copied from the twisted tattooing on his body. These tattoos had been done by a prophet who had worked out the complete explanation of heaven and earth. So Queequeg was a kind of walking riddle—a mystery story in one volume.

Carving Strange Drawings on the Coffin

The Old Blacksmith Makes a Harpoon.

CHAPTER 14

Strange Predictions

The *Pequod* had on board an old black-smith named Perth, and it was to him Ahab went to see about a special job. The captain brought the blacksmith a pouch of nailstubs from the shoes of racing horses and asked to have them melted down and made into an especially strong harpoon.

When Perth was about to give the sharp barb, or point, its final heating, he asked Ahab to bring the water cask to him. The cold water would temper, or harden, the barb. But Ahab had a different idea.

"No, I will not use water for that," said Ahab. "I want that harpoon point to be a true death weapon. It must be tempered in blood!" Then turning to the three Indians, he asked, "Tashtego, Queequeg, Daggoo, will ye give me as much blood as is needed to cover this point?"

The three men agreed, and three punctures were made in their skin. Soon the barb of the White Whale's harpoon was tempered... in human blood!

Later that night, Ahab awoke from a nightmare. He went up on deck where Fedallah was keeping watch and told him about his dream. In it, he saw himself in a hearse, a carriage for the dead.

Fedallah peered at him in the lantern's flickering glare. "I have told you my visions about the way you will die. Don't you remember? I said you will have neither a hearse nor a coffin."

A Harpoon Tempered in Blood!

"Yet I do worry," said Ahab. "People who die at sea do not have hearses."

"Aye, but did I not also say that before you could die on this trip, you would have to see two hearses on the sea?" Fedallah reminded him. "The first would not be made by human hands, and the second would be made of wood grown in America."

"That *would* be a strange sight on the ocean," said Ahab. "But what was that other saying about yourself?"

"That I would go before you, to pilot you into the other world.".

"And that after you die, Fedallah, you would again appear to me, to pilot me, right? Then I guess that means that I *will* be able to kill Moby Dick and live to tell the story."

"Here is another promise, old man," said the Indian mysteriously. "Only a *rope* can kill you."

"You must mean by hanging. But that can

Fedallah Predicts Ahab's Death.

never be." Ahab laughed mockingly. "Therefore, I am to live forever."

As we neared the equator—for it was there that Ahab hoped to find Moby Dick, we heard unearthly cries, like the wailing of ghosts. These cries were coming from the rocky islands past which we were sailing. The civilized part of the crew said it was mermaids, and the men shuddered. The pagan harpooners just kept calm. But the oldest sailor of all, who was from the Isle of Man, off the coast of England, had a different opinion. According to this old Manxman, we were hearing the voices of newly drowned men at sea.

Later on, when Flask told Ahab about the eerie sounds, the old man laughed. "I know all about those islands," he said. "It was just the cries of mother seals who have lost their cubs or the cries of cubs who have lost their mothers."

This explanation only made the crew feel

Unearthly Cries from a Rocky Island

worse. Most sailors are superstitious about seals. This is true not only because the animals' troubled tones sound human, but also because their round heads and half-intelligent faces resemble the heads and faces of humans. As a result, this was taken to be an evil omen, and the men fully expected something bad to happen.

Sure enough, the worst did happen—to a sailor who had climbed the mainmast to watch for the White Whale. Half-asleep, he had tumbled down into the sea. Immediately, the wooden life buoy was thrown overboard for him to cling to. But it had been in the sun too long and had dried out and shrunk. Water got into the wooden buoy, and the added weight of the water pulled it down, along with the poor sailor.

Now the men felt that the bad omen of the seals' cries has been fulfilled. But the old Manxman disagreed—that omen was not

A Life Buoy for a Drowning Man

fulfilled *yet*.

We needed to replace the buoy for future use, but we had trouble finding a light-enough cask from which to make it. Queequeg pointed to his coffin, offering its fine, hard wood as a replacement. The idea seemed strange to the officers at first, but finally they told the carpenter to nail the lid on tightly and seal the seams to make them waterproof. The *Pequod*'s life buoy now would be a coffin.

The next day, a large ship, the *Rachel*, came bearing down upon us, all her beams thickly clustered with men.

"Have ye seen the White Whale?" came Ahab's voice.

"Aye, yesterday. Have ye seen a whaleboat adrift?" came a voice from the *Rachel*.

In his joy that Moby Dick had been seen, Ahab didn't bother to reply and was interested only in boarding the *Rachel* to get more information. But her captain quickly got to

Queequeg Offers His Coffin as a Life Buoy.

our ship instead.

The captain of the *Rachel* answered Ahab's eager questions with an account of what had happened.

"Four of our boats went after the white hump of that whale, and the fastest one of them seemed to have fastened to him. Suddenly, both boat and whale disappeared, and we all figured that the wounded whale was running with his hunters. But though we searched all through the night, not the least glimpse of the missing boat was seen."

Ahab seemed disappointed, but the captain went on. "I've come on board to ask you to join us in the rescue search. We can sweep the area in parallel lines to search for my missing men, and...." He hesitated a moment, then went on. "You see, my own son is among them."

Here, the *Rachel's* captain noted Ahab's cold expression. "For God's sake, man, I am

The *Rachel*'s Captain Asks For Help.

begging you," he cried. "Let me hire your ship, then. I'll gladly pay."

"We must save the boy!" cried Stubb.

I was sure Stubb spoke for all of us on board, and the cries of approval from the men bore this out.

At that moment, the old Manxman raised his hand to silence everyone. "The boy drowned with the rest of them last night," he said. "Didn't we hear their spirits?"

Ahab ignored him, but turned to the captain and spoke calmly and coldly. "I will not do it. We are losing time right now. Good-bye and God bless ye, man."

The captain of the *Rachel* stood stunned for a moment.

Then Ahab turned to his First Mate and called, "Mr. Starbuck, in three minutes' time have all these strangers off and let the ship sail as before."

Ahab Refuses to Help.

"I've Got His Death Right Here!"

CHAPTER 15

The First Day's Chase

A few days later, we met another ship, badly misnamed the *Delight*. To Ahab's same burning question, the captain of the *Delight* replied by pointing to the splintered wreck of a whaleboat upon her beams.

"Have ye killed him?" asked Ahab.

"The harpoon has not been made yet that can do that, " said the captain of the *Delight*.

"I've got his death right here!" yelled Ahab, holding up his newly made harpoon.

"God help you then," cried the captain of the *Delight*. "I've lost five splendid men to that cursed White Whale! You are sailing on their tomb!"

In the past, Starbuck had repeatedly asked the old man to give up the mad chase for the hated White Whale. Again now, he pleaded with Ahab to turn back. "We have the cargo. Why not let the men return safely to the wives and their children?"

For a moment Ahab seemed to soften. He spoke longingly of his own wife and son. "My boy is waking now, sitting up in bed. And his mother is telling him about me, how I am at sea, but how I will return to play with him again." Ahab paused, then he added, "But there is some monster inside me pushing me on recklessly, making me do what I should not. No, Starbuck, I will never be content until I have killed the evil Moby Dick!"

At daybreak, Ahab sniffed the sea air and declared, "A whale is near."

Soon we all sensed the peculiar smell that

Captain Ahab's Family

the sperm whale gives off, and the old man rapidly changed the ship's course.

"I will make the first sighting of the whale myself," cried Ahab. "I must have the doubloon for sighting the whale first. Ahab *alone*!" And he pointed to the gold piece he'd nailed up long ago.

Ahab made a rope basket for himself and sat in it as two men hoisted him up to the mainmast for a full view of the sea. When he was about two-thirds of the way up, far higher than the other look-outs, he raised a cry like a sea gull, "There she blows—there she blows! A hump like a snow hill! It is Moby Dick!"

The men on deck rushed to the rigging for a glimpse of the famous whale they had been after so long. Moby Dick was there—a mile or so ahead. Every roll of the sea revealed his high sparkling hump and his silent spouts in the air.

"And did none of ye see him before?" cried

"There She Blows! It Is Moby Dick!"

Ahab to all the men perched around in the rigging.

"I did, almost that same instant, " said Tashtego, "and I cried out."

"Not the *same* instant, though," cried Ahab. "No, the doubloon is mine. Fate reserved it for me—for me *alone*! Only I could make Moby Dick appear!"

Ahab shouted orders in excitement. "Stand by, stand by! Lower me, Mr. Starbuck. Quicker, quicker! Get the boats ready." And he slid through the air to the deck.

Soon all the boats but Starbuck's were lowered, shooting ahead in the chase. Ahab saw only the wrinkles of the White Whale's head and the bright bubbles dancing playfully by his side. The broken pole of a whaler's lance still projected out of the White Whale's back. He seemed so calm and serene, but only because the terribleness of his jaw was hidden beneath the water. Suddenly, the whale

"The Doubloon Is Mine."

slowly rose up, forming a high white arch with his body. Then he waved his tail, almost as a warning, and swiftly dipped below the surface of the whirling pool he had just left.

The three boats floated in the stillness, awaiting the return of Moby Dick. Ahab peered over the side of his boat into the depths of the sea. A white living spot was rising quickly, revealing two long crooked rows of white, glistening teeth. It was Moby Dick's open mouth, yawning beneath Ahab's boat, looking like a marble burial room.

Ahab gave one sidelong sweep with his steering oar to whirl the boat around, away from the monstrous whale. This brought the bow round to face Moby Dick's head. But with the amazingly evil intelligence he seemed to possess, Moby Dick caught onto the plan. He cunningly ducked under and butted the boat with his head.

His long narrow jaw opened. Now he had

Moby Dick's Open Mouth Appears.

the bow in his mouth and one of his teeth caught in an oar-lock. The blue-white inside of his jaw was within six inches of Ahab's head when Moby Dick began to shake the boat gently, as a cat will do with a mouse in its jaws.

Fedallah sat still with his arms crossed, unafraid, while the rest of the crew tumbled over each other to reach the stern, away from the whale's open jaws.

Ahab, in a frenzy at being so close to getting his enemy but now helpless in its grasp, grabbed at the jawbone with his bare hands and tried to wrench it from its grip on the boat. But the jaw slipped from his grasp, and as it slid away, it came down on the boat like a huge pair of scissors and bit the boat completely in two!

The men were thrown into the water while Moby Dick angrily circled the area, churning up the water in his wake as if working himself up to another and more deadly attack.

Ahab Tries to Grab the Whale's Jaws.

The other boats hovered nearby, unharmed, still not daring to approach the tossing Ahab or the other crew members for fear of signaling another attack by the whale.

Luckily, the *Pequod* was able to sail between the whale and the swimming men. As Moby Dick sullenly swam off, the other boats flew to the rescue.

Ahab, half-blinded by the sea, was dragged into Stubb's boat. He struggled to his feet, crying, "Hands off me! The blood is running through my veins again. Set the sail! Man the oars! After the whale!"

But even with the added rowing power of the crew members just rescued, the boat could not match the speed of the whale. And Moby Dick sped away.

When everyone was finally back on board the *Pequod*, Ahab again spoke of the doubloon. "That gold is mine," he said. "I have earned it. But I will let it stay here until the

Ahab Is Dragged into Stubb's Boat.

White Whale is dead. Whichever of ye first sights him on the day he is killed, this gold is that man's. And if on that day I should again be the one to sight Moby Dick, then ten times that sum shall be divided among all of ye! Away now!"

And so saying, he took his position with his leg in the cutout opening on deck and stood there till the dawn, sleeping and rousing himself.

Thus ended the first day of the hunting of Moby Dick.

"The Gold Stays Here Until the Whale Is Dead."

"The Mad Fiend Himself Is After Ye!"

CHAPTER 16

The Second Day's Chase

The next day, the cry came again from the masthead, "There she blows—she blows!—she blows!—right ahead!"

"Aye, aye!" cried Stubb. "I knew it. Ye can't ecape! Blow on and split your pout, O whale. The mad fiend himself is after ye! Ahab will dam off your blood, as a miller shuts his water-gate upon the stream!"

The excitement of the chase had spread to all the crew. Whatever fears or forebodings they might have felt before were gone in their growing awe of Ahab, and the thirty men worked as one man toward the old captain's fatal goal.

Hardly had Ahab been hoisted to his high perch on the mast than a triumphant cry burst from thirty lungs on board. Less than a mile away, Moby Dick burst into view! Not by his calm, lazy spouting was he seen, but rather by his wondrous breaching—the tossing of his entire body out of the water and high into the air. This breaching was Moby Dick's act of defiance !

"There she breaches!" came the cry.

"Breach to the sun for your last time, Moby Dick!" cried Ahab. "Your time has come! My harpoon is ready! The boats—stand by!"

Ahab dropped from his perch and onto the deck. "Lower away!" he cried as soon as he reached his boat.

As if to strike terror into them by being the first to attack, Moby Dick had turned and now headed straight for the three whaleboats.

This time Ahab headed straight for the

Moby Dick's Act of Defiance!

MOBY DICK

White Whale's forehead, because the animal sees better from the sides than from the front. But before they could reach him, and while all three boats were still within the whale's sight, Moby Dick churned himself into a furious speed. With open jaws and lashing tail, he rushed among the boats. Ignoring the irons darting into him from every boat, he crossed and recrossed, tangling all the lines.

Caught and twisted in the mazes of lines, harpoons, and lances, Moby Dick came flashing and dripping up to the very bow of Ahab's boat. There was only one thing for the old man to do—cut his line loose. But as he did so, the White Whale made a sudden rush among the remaining tangled lines. This pulled the boats of Stubb and Flask towards him, dashing them together, then overturning them like roaring waves would do to two sea shells. Then the whale dove down into the sea, disappearing in a boiling whirlpool.

Overturning the Boats

The two crews frantically circled in the waters, with Flask bobbing up and down like an empty bottle, twitching his legs upward to escape the dreaded jaws of the whale, and with Stubb calling out to be ladled up.

Ahab was about to head into the whirlpool to rescue those whom he could when his boat suddenly shot up from the sea. It moved as if pulled skyward by invisible wires. Moby Dick had dashed his broad forehead against the bottom of Ahab's boat and sent it spinning over and over in the air. Finally it landed, upside down, and Ahab and his men struggled out from under it.

Soon, as if satisfied with his work for the time being, the whale pushed his forehead through the ocean, trailing after him the intertangled lines.

As before, the *Pequod* bore down to the rescue and dropped a boat for the floating crewmen, their oars, and their harpoons. Ahab

Moby Dick Sends Ahab's Boat Spinning.

was picked up clinging to his boat's broken half. Luckily, there were no fatalities, only bad cuts and sprained shoulders, wrists, and ankles.

Back on the deck of the *Pequod*, Ahab half-hung on Starbuck's shoulder. His ivory leg had been snapped off, leaving one short sharp splinter.

"Old Ahab is untouched!" he cried. "Not even a broken bone. Here, give me that lance for a cane, then gather the men together."

When the crew had gathered before him, Ahab searched the faces for one man— Fedallah. But the Manillan was nowhere!

"Aye, sir," said Stubb. "He was caught among the tangles of your line. I thought I saw him being dragged under."

"*My* line! *My* line? Gone? That is an omen of death—*my* death!" cried Ahab. "Quick! Collect all the irons now. If I have to go around this globe ten times, aye, or even dive straight

Ahab's Ivory Leg Has Been Snapped Off.

through it, I will slay Moby Dick yet! "

"Great God!" cried Starbuck. "You will never capture him, old man. No more of this! It's madness. For two days you chased him, and for two days our boats were broken to splinters. Your very leg was snatched from under you. You've had enough warnings. Must we chase this murderous fish till he drags every last one of us to the bottom of the sea?"

"This whole act was decreed a billion years before this ocean rolled," cried Ahab. "Laugh, my men. 'Tis said that drowning things rise twice to the surface, then rise again to sink for evermore. So with Moby Dick. Two days he's floated. Tomorrow will be the third—he'll rise once more—only to spout his last!"

Then to himself, Ahab muttered, "Fedallah had predicted he would go before me. But he said I would see him once again before I die. Now *there's* a riddle to baffle my brain, but one that I will solve."

Starbuck Pleads with Ahab.

"I Meet Thee This Third Time, Moby Dick!"

CHAPTER 17

The Strange Prediction Comes True

The morning of the third day dawned fair. Once again the lone night look-out on the masthead was relieved by crowds of daylight look-outs who dotted every mast.

With a quickly made wooden leg to replace the lost ivory one, Ahab was again hoisted up the mast in his rope basket. After an hour of searching the sea, he spied the spout. Three shrieks of "There she blows!" went up from the mastheads.

"Forehead to forehead I meet thee this third time, Moby Dick!" called Ahab. Then, patting the masthead lovingly, he added, "Good-bye, masthead. I'm going down. Keep a good eye on the whale while I'm gone. We'll talk tomorrow, no tonight, when the White Whale lies down there, tied by head and tail."

As Ahab was being lowered, the riddle came back to his thoughts. He whispered to himself, "But what was it that Fedallah said? He would go before me, yet he would be seen again. But where? I've sailed far from where he sank. No, Fedallah, you may have been right in your prediction for yourself, but you were wrong about Ahab!"

As Ahab prepared to climb into his boat, he turned to Starbuck. "Shake hands with me, man. I am old, very old."

His eyes filling with tears, Starbuck pleaded, "Oh, my captain, do not go! A brave man weeps and begs you."

"Lower away!" cried Ahab, shaking his mate's arm from him.

"Oh, My Captain, Do Not Go!"

The boats were lowered, but they had not gone far when a signal from the masthead, a downward-pointed arm, told Ahab the whale had gone down.

As the waves hammered on the bow of his boat, Ahab cried, "Beat on, beat on! I'm not afraid. I shall be there when Moby Dick rises. Oh, Fedallah, you were wrong. There will be no coffin and no hearse for me. Remember, only a *rope* can kill me! Ha! Ha!"

Suddenly the waters around them swirled and swelled in broad circles. A low rumbling sound was heard. Everyone held their breaths as trailing ropes, harpoons, lances, and finally the whale shot up from the sea.

Maddened by the previous day's fresh irons in him, Moby Dick came head-on, angrily churning his tail among the boats, spilling out irons, and dashing in part of their bows.

As the whale turned and shot by them again, a cry went up. Lashed to the whale's

Moby Dick Attacks Head-On.

back, amid the tangled ropes was the half-torn body of Fedallah! His opened eyes were turned full upon old Ahab!

The harpoon dropped from the captain's hand, and he drew in a long breath. "So thou spoke true, Fedallah," he whispered. "And now I do see thee again after thy death. And thy prediction about thy hearse was right too. Aye, the hearse was not made by human hands. Thy hearse is Moby Dick... ! But where is the second hearse?" Ahab eyed his restless crew.

"Down, men!" he cried. "The first one that tries to jump from this boat I'm in, him I will harpoon. Ye are not other men; ye are my arms and my legs, and so ye will obey me. Now where's that whale?"

Moby Dick swam away from the boats at top speed and on his way out to sea. Ahab turned to follow. He was just passing the *Pequod* when Starbuck called down from the

Fedallah's Half-Torn Body!

deck.

"Oh, Ahab, it is not too late to turn back. See! Moby Dick is not after you. It is you, you, that is madly after *him*!"

But Ahab commanded his boat to continue to follow the whale. Glancing up at his ship, he saw Tashtego, Queequeg, and Daggoo eagerly climbing to the three mastheads. He saw the oarsmen working on the two damaged boats which had been hoisted to the *Pequod*'s side. Through the portholes as he sped by, he caught flying glimpses of Stubb and Flask, busy among bundles of new irons and lances.

Ahab's oarsmen had trouble rowing. Sharks had gathered around his boat and were biting at the oars with every dip.

"Pay them no mind," cried Ahab. "Those teeth are only rowlocks for your oars. Pull on!"

"But, sir, at every bite the blades grow smaller and smaller."

"They will last long enough. Pull on! Do

Sharks Bite at the Oars.

these sharks expect to feast on the whale or
or old Ahab?"

When they were alongside the White
Whale's flank, the smoky mist from his spout
curled around them. Ahab arched his body
back and with both arms raised, he darted
his fierce iron and his even fiercer curse into
the hated Moby Dick!

The White Whale writhed and rolled his
flank against the small boat, turning it partly
over. Three crewmen were tossed into the
sea, but Ahab clung to the raised side and
stayed inside the boat.

As the whale darted off into the sea, Ahab
yelled to the men to hold the line fastened to
Moby Dick. But the line could not withstand
the strain, and it snapped in the empty air!

As Moby Dick turned, he spied the black
hull of the *Pequod*. Thinking maybe it was the
cause of all his trouble, he bore down on its
oncoming prow with his jaws ready to strike.

Ahab Darts His Iron into Moby Dick.

"The whale! The ship!" cried the cringing oarsmen.

"The ship, the ship! Tilt, tilt, O sea! Let Ahab slide the last time downward on his prey. Dash on, my men! Will ye not save my ship?" shouted Ahab wildly.

On board the *Pequod,* men stared, babbled, prayed—their enchanted eyes fixed upon the whale that was rushing straight toward them.

"Oh, Ahab!" cried Starbuck. "Look at thy work. The whale drives toward us. My God, stand by me now. The grinning whale prepares to gulp us all!"

Moby Dick's solid white forehead smashed the ship's starboard bow with vengeance. Men shook and fell flat on their faces as mountain torrents of water began pouring in through the break.

"The second hearse! The ship itself is the second hearse!" cried Ahab, looking up from his boat. "Its wood could only be American!

The Whale's Forehead Smashes into the Bow.

Aye, those were Fedallah's words—a hearse made from American wood."

The whale turned away from the sinking ship, dove beneath its keel, and came up quietly a few yards from Ahab's boat. He lay there, unmoving, for a time.

"I turn my body from the sun," cried Ahab. "O *Pequod*, my death-glorious ship. Must ye then perish and sink without me? Am I cut off from a captain's pride—going down with my ship? How lonely is my death after such a lonely life! I roll towards thee, thou all-destroying but unconquering whale. To the last I shall fight thee! In hate I shall spit my last breath at thee! Tow me to pieces while I chase thee, tied to thee, damned whale! *Thus* I give up the spear! "

With all the power in him, Ahab hurled the harpoon. The stricken whale darted forward with lightning speed, tangling the harpoon's line with a jerk. As Ahab stooped to untangle

"To the Last I Shall Fight Thee!"

it, a turn of the rope caught him round the neck, and he was shot out of the boat. Before the crew knew what was happening, he was gone...killed by a rope!

For an instant, the crewmen stood still, as in a trance. They they turned. "The ship? Great God, where is the *Pequod*?"

Through the mist they saw the *Pequod* fading into the sea, the faithful harpooners still maintaining the look-outs on her high masts. Then a whirlpool of water seized the only remaining boat and spun it about round and round until all its crew, every oar, every lance pole, every floating chip of the *Pequod*—everything was carried to the bottom of the ocean.

And the great White Whale sped away.

And the sea rolled on as it had been rolling for five thousand years....

A Turn of the Rope Catches Ahab.

Queequeg's Coffin Bursts from the Whirlpool.

CHAPTER 18

I Alone Survived

The story's done, and I alone survived the wreck.

As I was being pulled round and round toward the center of the whirlpool, a black bubble shot up from its center and burst. A coffin-shaped life buoy burst from the bubble and floated by my side. Even after death, my best friend had saved my life. It was Queequeg's coffin-buoy.

I floated on it one whole day and one whole night. The sharks did me no harm as they glided by, and the savage sea hawks sailed right over me with their beaks shut tightly.

I had much to think about during those solitary sea-borne hours. I thought of Ahab's drive unto death, and of the White Whale's answering fierceness. And the memory of Queequeg's kindness buoyed my spirits, just as his chest now held my body afloat.

The second day, a sail drew near, nearer, and picked me up at last. It was the wandering *Rachel*, still looking for her missing children. But she found only me, Ishmael, another orphan.

The *Rachel* Rescues Ishmael.